For my grandson, Burhan,
and
Casey and Max Fleming

LIBRARY OF CONGRESS CATALOGING-IN-PUBLICATION DATA

Demi, author, illustrator.

[Fables. Selections]

The pandas and their chopsticks : and other animals stories / written
and illustrated by Demi.

pages cm

Summary: Presents ten animal stories, each containing a moral lesson,
including the importance of being humble, the dangers of being too
proud, the importance of generosity and sharing, and how everyone, no
matter how small, has a part to play in life.

ISBN 978-1-937786-16-8 (hardcover : alk. paper) 1. Fables, American.
2. Children's stories, American. [1. Fables. 2. Short stories.] I.
Title.

PZ8.2.D3Pan 2014

[E]--dc23

2014010104

The illustrations are rendered in mixed media
Book design by Michael Nelson
Printed on acid-free paper in China
Production Date: April 2014
Plant & Location: Printed by 1010 International, Co. Ltd
Job / Batch # TT14030096

For information address Wisdom Tales,
P.O. Box 2682, Bloomington, Indiana 47402-2682
www.wisdomtalespress.com

the Pandas and their Chopsticks

AND OTHER
ANIMAL STORIES

•Wisdom Tales•

WRITTEN
AND ILLUSTRATED
BY
Demi

THE PANDAS AND THEIR CHOPSTICKS

Once there was a very curious panda. One day as he was playing outside, he heard angry sounds. They came from a big house, so he looked inside the window. There he saw a large group of pandas. They were all seated around a huge table. They were growling and snapping at each other. On the table there were many dishes of bamboo shoots—the pandas' favorite food! Beside each panda was a pair of chopsticks. But the chopsticks were three feet long! The pandas were getting madder and hungrier every minute. The curious panda saw why: Not one of them could figure out how to eat with their three-foot-long chopsticks!

The curious panda continued playing out-side. All of a sudden he heard happy sounds coming from a big house, so he looked inside the window. There he saw another large group of pandas. But these pandas were laughing and smiling. They, too, were seated around a huge table. And this table also had many dishes of bamboo shoots on it. Each panda also had chop-sticks that were three feet long. But these pandas were getting happier and fuller every minute. The curious panda smiled when he saw why: They were all feeding one another across the table with their three-foot-long chopsticks!

Be generous.
It brings happiness to everyone.

THE CAT WHO PRAYED

A cat with prayer beads around his neck was sitting quietly. His eyes seemed tightly shut.

Two mice saw him and were very surprised.

"That old cat has surely changed his ways," they said. "He has started praying. Now we don't have to worry about him anymore!"

The mice thought they were very lucky. They jumped up and down, and began to play. They paid no attention to the cat.

Suddenly, the sly cat jumped at them and almost ate them up. The terrified mice ran home as fast as they could. They said to each other, "We won't be tricked like that again!"

Be careful around those who make a show of how good they are.

THE FOX
WHO WAS KING
OF THE FOREST

One day a tiger was hunting in the forest. He caught a fox and was ready to eat him.

But the fox quickly said, "You must not eat me. I am the King of the Forest. Don't you know of my incredible powers? Come with me. Let me show you how the animals fear me!"

All the other animals saw the fox coming. But behind him they also saw the huge tiger. Terrified, they ran away as fast as they could.

"I see what you mean," said the tiger. "I'd better find something else to eat." And away he went.

The weaker you are, the smarter you have to be.

A HEDGEHOG THINKS TWICE

A hedgehog lost his favorite shovel. He was sure the thief was the hedgehog who lived next door. Everything about my neighbor proves he has stolen the shovel, thought the hedgehog. Just look at the way he scurries about and listen to all the noises he makes!

A little while later the suspicious hedgehog went to the garden for some turnips. He was surprised to find his shovel right where he had forgotten it!

Then when he looked at his neighbor again, nothing about him looked like a thief.

Be very careful with your thoughts.
They can make false things seem true.

THE HELPFUL HUMMINGBIRD

One day when a mighty elephant was walking along, it saw a tiny hummingbird lying on its back. It had its tiny feet up in the air.

"What's the matter with you?" asked the mighty elephant.

"I heard that the heavens are going to fall today!" said the hummingbird.

The mighty elephant laughed. "Do you think your tiny feet could hold up all the heavens?"

The tiny hummingbird replied, "Maybe they couldn't hold all of it up. But I'm sure they could hold up a piece!"

Great things can be done when everyone, no matter how small, does their part.

THE TURTLE WHO COULDN'T STOP TALKING

Long ago there was a turtle who couldn't stop talking. He had two friends that were cranes. They lived happily together by a lovely lake.

One year there was no rain. The lake had dried up.

"We must fly to Heavenly Lake," said the cranes.

"But how?" asked the turtle. "I don't have wings!"

"We could fly you there. But you must promise to keep your mouth shut. You cannot say a word to anybody!"

"I can do that!" said the turtle.

And so the cranes found a strong stick. They held the ends in their beaks. The turtle gripped the middle of the stick with his mouth. Then they were ready to go. The cranes flew up into the air. The turtle was between them, holding tightly onto the stick.

As they flew along, some children looked up. "See that silly turtle up in the air! Have you ever seen anything like that?"

The children all began to laugh at him. The turtle's pride was deeply hurt. He started to say, "I'm not silly. . ."

But as soon as he opened his mouth, the proud turtle started to fall. He fell into the lake far below with a great big splash.

Pride often opens our mouths.
Humility tells us when to keep them closed.

THE FROG WHO COUNTED TWO STARS FROM THE BOTTOM OF HIS WELL

A frog once lived in a very small well. One day, a big turtle passed by. He had come all the way from the great sea.

When the frog saw the turtle, he called out. "Come on down and look how good life is for me here! I can hop along the sides of my well. I can lie in the cool soft mud below. And at night I can see two stars!"

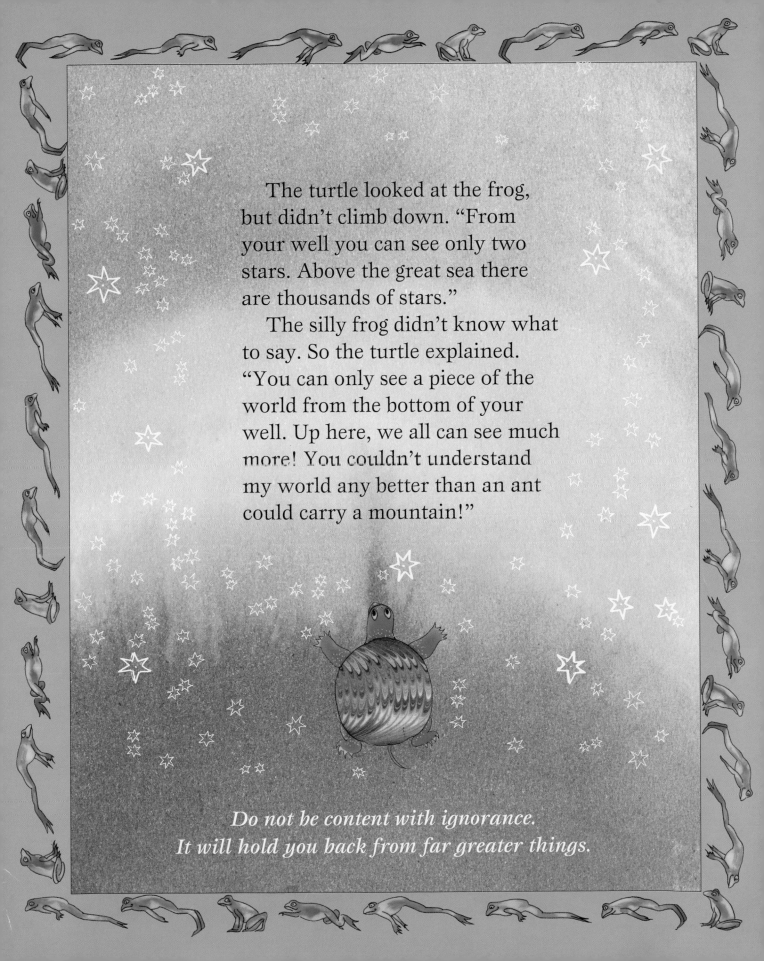

The turtle looked at the frog, but didn't climb down. "From your well you can see only two stars. Above the great sea there are thousands of stars."

The silly frog didn't know what to say. So the turtle explained. "You can only see a piece of the world from the bottom of your well. Up here, we all can see much more! You couldn't understand my world any better than an ant could carry a mountain!"

Do not be content with ignorance.
It will hold you back from far greater things.

THE KITE
ON A STRING

One day a kite on a string was allowed to fly very high. It sailed way above the clouds.

The happy kite called out to a butterfly below. "Hello butterfly! I am so much higher than you! Aren't you just a little bit jealous of me?"

"Jealous? Not at all," called out the butterfly.

The kite was surprised, and a little disappointed.

"You shouldn't show off!" continued the butterfly. "You can fly very high, it is true. But look, you are always tied to a string. You can only fly where the owner of the kite wants you to fly. I know that I cannot fly very high. But I can fly wherever and whenever I want to fly!"

He who boasts a lot achieves little.

THE OWL'S HOOT

A dove met an owl.
"Where are you off to?" asked the dove.
"I am moving to the east," replied the owl.
"Why are you moving?" asked the dove.
"The birds here don't like the sound of my hoot," the owl replied.

A few days later the dove met the owl again. The dove asked, "Where are you off to now?"

The owl said, "The birds in the east don't like the sound of my hoot. Nor do the birds in the west, the north, and the south. So, I've decided to fly to Heaven."

"Wouldn't it be much better," suggested the dove, "if you just changed your hoot? Otherwise even in Heaven no one will like the way you sound."

Our faults follow us wherever we go, unless we do something to leave them behind.

A RIVER DISCOVERS THE OCEAN

Once upon a time, there was a big river. The river was so wide that buffaloes on one bank couldn't see horses on the other. The big river was proud. He thought that he was as great as great could be.

Imagine his surprise when he finally came to the ocean. It was so much bigger than himself!

The river said to the ocean, "If I hadn't seen your size with my own eyes, I wouldn't have believed it. I thought I was as great as great could be!"

The ocean replied, "Nothing on earth is as great as me. Thousands of rivers flow into me, yet I am never full. But I know I am still just one part of the earth. And I am still only a speck of dust compared to the greatness of Heaven!"

Be humble.
It is the starting point of all greatness.